About this Book

Danger at Demon's Cove is an exciting adventure that takes you on an ancient trail in search of the amazing Demon's Eye Diamond and lost treasure.

Throughout the book, there are lots of tricky puzzles and perplexing problems which you must solve in order to understand the next part of the story.

Look at the pictures carefully and watch out for vital clues and information. Sometimes you will need to flick back through the book to help you find an answer. There are extra clues on page 41 and you can check the answers on pages 42 to 48.

Just turn the page to begin the adventure . . .

Sally

Max

Max and Sally are on holiday. They are camping outside their grandparents' house on the cliff top above Demon's Cove. Between them, they manage to find all the clues and solve the mystery. Can you?

3

A Dark and Stormy Night

It was a dark and stormy night, long ago. A ship called the Indian Queen was on her way home from the East, loaded with spices and silk. There was also a secret cargo belonging to a fabulously rich prince which Captain T. Clipper had pledged to guard with his life – an amazing hoard of treasure, including the Demon's Eye, a huge, priceless, black diamond.

The Indian Queen was lashed by fierce waves. The Captain struggled to steer the ship and desperately looked out for the lighthouse beam.

Meanwhile, the three evil Grabbitt brothers waited on the cliffs above Demon's Cove, sending a false signal to lure the ship onto the rocks.

The Captain spotted the signal. The doomed Indian Queen unwittingly sailed onto the treacherous rocks and began sinking fast.

Denzil, Jago and Joshua Grabbitt eagerly hauled the cargo onto the shore, without a thought for the crew of the wrecked ship.

The Indian Queen sank without trace, while the brothers inspected their booty. Denzil, the most evil of them, prised open the chests.

The greedy Grabbitts stared incredulously at the glittering jewels and amazing treasure, hardly able to believe their luck at such a haul.

DANGER AT DEMON'S COVE

Karen Dolby

Illustrated by Graham Round

Designed by
Graham Round and Brian Robertson

Series Editor: Gaby Waters

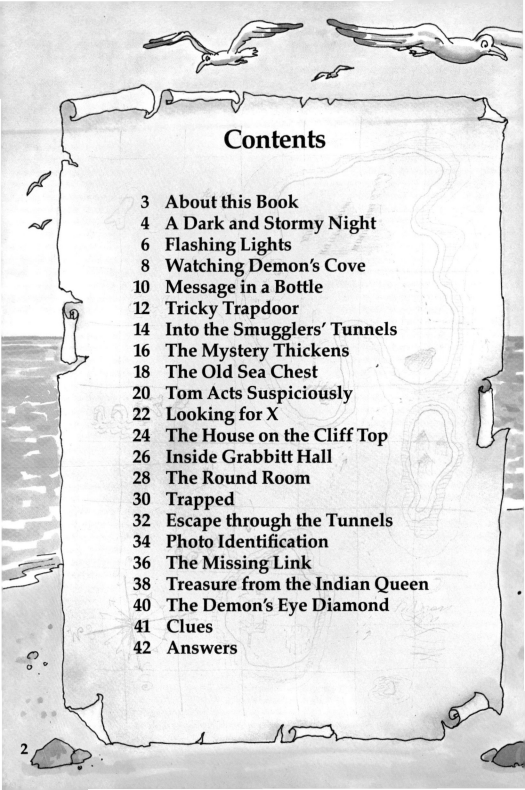

Contents

Tom paused and gazed out to sea. Sally shivered. She could picture it all clearly.

"But what happened to the treasure?" asked Max. "What did the Grabbitts do with it?"

"It's said that they hid the two treasure chests in the maze of smugglers' tunnels at Demon's Cove," Tom continued. "But within months the brothers had mysteriously perished and the secret of the treasure was lost with them.

Some say the Demon's Eye diamond held a curse. No one knows for sure. But even now, ghostly cries are heard echoing through the caves and on stormy nights the phantom Indian Queen can be seen sailing in the bay at Demon's Cove."

Flashing Lights

Later that night, Max and Sally were asleep in their tent on the cliffs above Demon's Cove. A sudden loud roar of thunder woke Sally with a start.

She peered out through the tent flap as lightning lit up the bay. Sally rubbed her eyes in disbelief. Was this the ghostly Indian Queen . . . ?

Then the flashing lights began and she realized it was a modern boat. By now Max was awake and they watched as a series of long and short flashes beamed across the bay.

"Perhaps it's a signal," said Max, as a lorry drew up on the cliff top opposite.

Sally quickly grabbed a notebook and started to scribble down the sequence, using dots for short flashes and dashes for long flashes. Max rummaged through a bag stuffed with useful equipment and pulled out his pocket codebook. He flicked through it until he found the page he was looking for and handed it to Sally.

"This will help us work out what it means," he said.

DON'T TURN THE PAGE YET

Can you decode the signal?

7

Watching Demon's Cove

Snatching a torch, Sally and Max hurried outside. Halfway down the steps to the cove, there was a wide ledge where they could hide and watch the beach.

A small dinghy pulled ashore. Two men clambered out and glared around, suspiciously. They began unloading some large, wooden crates. What was going on? Were they smugglers? Max leant out to get a better look and dislodged an avalanche of stones and pebbles.

They crouched down as a torch beam flashed in their direction, scanning the rock face again and again. They waited, hearts pounding, until at last a gruff voice gave the all clear.

Sally and Max stayed well hidden behind the rocks. They couldn't risk being discovered now. They heard muffled voices fading into the distance, but could see nothing. Soon there was silence and, in spite of the cold, they both felt very sleepy…

Max woke suddenly, sunlight dazzling him. He jumped to his feet, but the people and dinghy had vanished. He shook Sally and dashed down to the beach.

Max thought he caught a glimpse of the boat, but Sally was puzzled by the footprints. She could see three sets of tracks heading in one direction towards the cliff where they stopped. Someone must have rowed the dinghy away, but where had the other three people gone?

Sally stared at the cliff face, looking for a clue. She thought back to last night. Something had changed.

DON'T TURN THE PAGE YET

What has Sally noticed?

9

Message in a Bottle

Sally stared up towards the large boulder, sure it was hiding something. She took a deep breath and jumped onto the rocks. She scrambled up to the wide, grassy ledge with Max struggling behind.

Sally leant against the boulder and pushed. It was surprisingly light and rolled away to reveal a narrow opening. Max peered into the gloomy darkness. Sally flicked on the torch and they stepped cautiously through the gap to investigate.

They found themselves in a small cave. The torch beam disturbed some bats, but otherwise the cave was empty. Footprints in the sand matched the ones on the beach and showed that three people had walked into, but not out of, the cave. So where had they gone?

"Perhaps there's a secret tunnel," said Max.

Sally began tapping the walls, but they felt disappointingly solid. Max looked for hidden levers or buttons. But they found nothing.

Suddenly, Sally spotted a block of stone that had been firmly wedged into the wall. After a lot of tugging and a final wrench that sent Max tumbling backwards, they pulled it free and stared into the hole at an old, cobwebby bottle. Sally lifted it from its hiding place and Max pulled out a crumbly roll of paper. It was torn at the edges and faded by damp and age, but they could still see the clear outlines of a map and peculiar, sloping writing that was almost impossible to read.

DON'T TURN THE PAGE YET

Can you work out what the writing says?

Tricky Trapdoor

Sally studied the paper, thinking hard about what it meant. This was only part of a map and she wondered what had happened to the rest of it. She was sure the map was important, why else would Jago Grabbitt have hidden it so carefully? Could it have something to do with the treasure from the Indian Queen?

Max scuffed his way across the floor, searching for signs of a trapdoor. Suddenly he caught his foot in a ring half buried in the ground and tripped, knocking over a heavy, metal pole. He lay sprawled on the floor, but at least he knew where the trapdoor was.

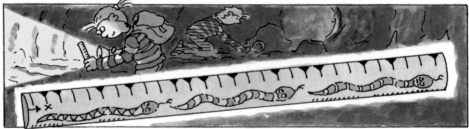

Just then, Sally noticed an unusual, carved stick lying on a rock. She tucked it into her bag, then began to help Max brush away the sand from a heavy, old, oak door.

The rusty, metal ring was embedded in one side of the trapdoor. Max lifted up the ring and tugged.

Together, Sally and Max heaved, pulled and yanked, but still they couldn't lift it. The door wouldn't budge.

They gave up, this was getting them nowhere. There HAD to be another way of opening the trapdoor. Max gazed around the cave searching for inspiration, but there didn't seem to be anything that would help. Then he had a brainwave.

"This should be easy," Max exclaimed, confidently. "I know how to open it."

DON'T TURN THE PAGE YET

How can they open the trapdoor?

Into the Smugglers' Tunnels

Eek! It's dark down here.

I know, stupid. Hurry up and find the torch.

Sally stepped onto the rickety ladder and began to clamber down. Max followed gingerly. But just at that moment, the ladder wobbled. CRASH! The trapdoor slammed shut, plunging them into darkness. They were trapped and had no choice but to go on.

At the bottom, Sally flicked on her torch. The beam barely pierced the blackness. They tried to match their route with Jago's map, but before long they were hopelessly lost.

On and on, they crawled and climbed through dank, dripping tunnels and echoing, shadowy caves. Sometimes they thought they could hear voices, but they saw no one. At last, Max saw a steep flight of steps leading up to a small trapdoor. It creaked as they pushed against it, but opened easily.

As she peered out, Sally gasped, "I know where we are."

DON'T TURN THE PAGE YET

Where are Max and Sally?

The Mystery Thickens

Silence. The cottage was deserted. Max and Sally pushed open the trapdoor and scrambled out.

They gazed at the cluttered room. Every corner and shelf was crammed with an odd assortment of curios collected from around the world. But there were also several puzzling things that seemed very unlikely possessions for a fisherman like Tom.

Suddenly, something made Sally stop and stare, a name she remembered from Tom's story of the Indian Queen.

DON'T TURN THE PAGE YET

What has Sally spotted?

The Old Sea Chest

Max tried the chest. It was unlocked. Sally looked doubtful; she didn't like the idea of snooping through someone else's things.

"There's something going on, and I want to find out what," said Max.

The chest was packed with mementoes from the Indian Queen – the Captain's logbook, ancient charts and old doubloons and pieces of eight . . . Max tried out the telescope, but it didn't work. He just stared into luminous, inky, blackness.

Then a recent newspaper cutting caught his eye. Max was certain he had seen the man in the photo before. He racked his brains trying to remember where.

As he read and reread the stories, a worrying suspicion began to grow in his mind. Everything that had happened started to make sense.

DON'T TURN THE PAGE YET

Where has Max seen the man before? What does he suspect?

Ship's Log

Nov. 10th. Took on freshe water and supplyes. Our scurvey sufferers seeme greatly cheered. A fayre wind is behinde us and full sails are set. Offered two guineas reward for first sight of lande.

Nov. 11th. Made goode speed during the night but now the barometer is fallyng and the wind has changed to a Sou' Westerly direction. We are in for a blow. The crewe seeme cheerfull and long to be home.

Nov. 12th. Barometer still fallyng. Have battened downe the hatches and furled the mainsail. Never have I felte

suche a gale, nor seene suche waves. Doubled the men's grog rationes to keep them in goode spirits.

Nov. 13th. Weather still worseninge. Bosun Smollett sighted lande firste, but 'tis an evill night. I feare he will never collect his two guineas, nore will we see our homes againe.

All is last, we are wrecked. The shippe is being torn apart. I must secure my speciall charge.... Place one's eye to the eye-piece, where the eye shall see nowt but the Eye.

FREE AGAIN

From our man in Cairo

Two members of the notorious Doppel Gang were released yesterday without charge, following the reappearance of the famous six-toed Lost Idol.

They are Gloria Goldfinger, jet-setter and collector of expensive jewellery, and John Smith, alias Luigi Macaroni, Hans Sauerkraut and other names – a ruthless master of disguise.

Both wore dark glasses and John sported a new beard, as they boarded a private plane last night with top lawyer, Eustace Whimpe, bound for an unknown destination.

DARING HELICOPTER JAILBREAK

At dawn this morning, another member of the Doppel Gang, Silas 'Spikey' Scarface, was airlifted from Turnquay prison where he

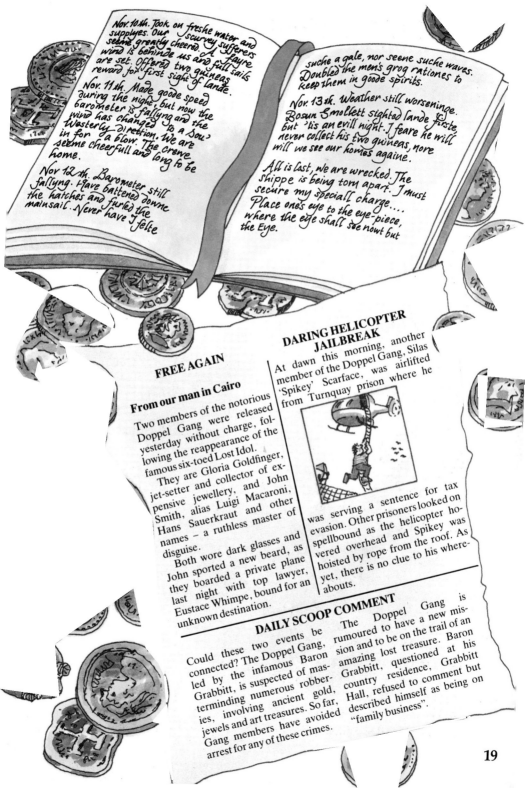

was serving a sentence for tax evasion. Other prisoners looked on spellbound as the helicopter hovered overhead and Spikey was hoisted by rope from the roof. As yet, there is no clue to his whereabouts.

DAILY SCOOP COMMENT

Could these two events be connected? The Doppel Gang, led by the infamous Baron Grabbitt, is suspected of masterminding numerous robberies, involving ancient gold, jewels and art treasures. So far, Gang members have avoided arrest for any of these crimes. The Doppel Gang is rumoured to have a new mission and to be on the trail of an amazing lost treasure. Baron Grabbitt, questioned at his country residence, Grabbitt Hall, refused to comment but described himself as being on "family business".

Tom Acts Suspiciously

THUD THUD THUD…

Sally and Max slowly repacked the chest, their heads buzzing with unanswered questions.

Had they been watching the infamous Doppel Gang at Demon's Cove last night? Was the Gang searching for the lost treasure from the Indian Queen? And what was Tom's part in all this? It was very suspicious.

Heavy footsteps came closer and closer until they stopped outside the front door. Sally and Max watched in horror as the handle slowly turned. What should they do now? Max scooted into the open trapdoor. Sally shut the chest and dived behind the sofa, hardly daring to breathe as Tom sat down in it. She was trapped.

The silence was broken by a strange, crackling sound, followed by a high-pitched whine. Sally cautiously peeped out over the sofa as Tom leapt to his feet and rushed across to the radio.

He sat down at his desk, adjusted the radio and listened intently through the headphones. He was writing something down and seemed to be checking a notebook.

Max opened the trapdoor and saw a carved stick drop to the floor. It was the same size and just like the one Sally had picked up.

Minutes, later the door banged shut and Tom's brisk footsteps faded into the distance. Sally and Max emerged from hiding.

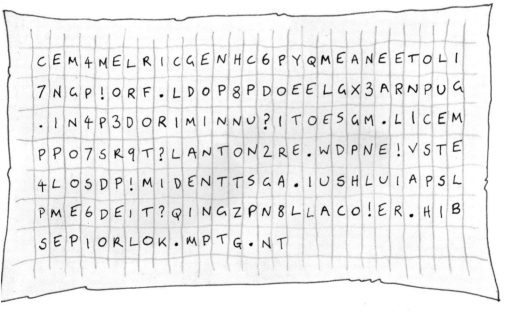

```
C E M 4 M E L R I C G E N H C 6 P Y Q M E A N E E T O L I
7 N G P ! O R F . L D O P 8 P D O E E L G X 3 A R N P U G
. I N 4 P 3 D O R I M I N N U ? I T O E 5 G M . L I C E M
P P O 7 S R 9 T ? L A N T O N 2 R E . W D P N E ! V S T E
4 L O S D P ! M I D E N T T S G A . I U S H L U I A P S L
P M E 6 D E I T ? Q I N G Z P N 8 L L A C O ! E R . H I B
S E P I O R L O K . M P T G . N T
```

The paper Tom had been writing on was lying on his desk next to the radio. He had neatly written seven rows of letters on the squared paper, but they didn't appear to mean anything. Sally was totally puzzled.

"It's a code," said Max. "And I know how to read it."

DON'T TURN THE PAGE YET

What does the message say?

Looking for X

The message confirmed their worst suspicions, but where WAS the usual meeting place? Max slumped down into a chair. All their detective work seemed to have come to nothing.

Then Sally spotted Tom's notebook lying on top of the radio. It was open at a map marked with a red cross. Could this be the meeting place? It was a long shot, but it had to be worth trying. It was their only lead.

There were no labels, but Sally was sure it was a map of Nether Muckle. She and Max ran outside to the back of the cottage and stared at the village. If only they could match the map to the roads and buildings.

DON'T TURN THE PAGE YET

Can you work out which building is the one marked X on the map?

The House on the Cliff Top

Max and Sally sprinted through the village and ran on along the cliff road, past the Smuggler's Head Hotel and ruined abbey. Finally, they turned into the lane leading to the strange house on the cliff's edge.

The steep hill in front of the house made a good viewpoint. Max and Sally scrambled to the top using the thick gorse bushes as cover. Gasping for breath, they crawled to the edge and stared down at Grabbitt Hall, home of Baron Grabbitt. If this was the meeting place, they had to get inside, but finding a way in would be tricky.

DON'T TURN THE PAGE YET

Can you find a safe route into Grabbitt Hall?

24

Inside Grabbitt Hall

The meeting is in the round room at the end of the passage leading off the drawing room. You know the entry procedure.

Grabbitt Hall was ominously quiet. Max and Sally sneaked downstairs and along a deserted corridor. Now they had to find out where the meeting was being held, without being discovered.

Max and Sally heard the buzz of voices ahead. They ducked behind a large suit of armour and peered out. A man was standing in the hallway giving directions to two familiar-looking people.

They waited impatiently for the man to walk slowly away down a flight of stairs and then silently tiptoed after the two visitors. Sally and Max turned into a wide, blue-carpeted corridor in time to see them disappearing through a doorway.

A minute later, Max turned the doorhandle and peeped into the room. It was empty. He looked for a door or passage, but the only door was this one. It was very strange, there HAD to be another way out. The two visitors couldn't have vanished into thin air.

Sally looked around. The walls were covered with portraits of the Baron's Grabbitt ancestors. But something was puzzling Max. Looking at one of the paintings, he could see the room had hardly changed over the years, but one thing was different. What was it?

"I've got it," Max exclaimed. "There's a secret passage, and I know where it is."

DON'T TURN THE PAGE YET

What has Max spotted? Where is the door to the secret passage?

The Round Room

Max stood face to face with the portrait of Baron Grabbitt.

"He's not very friendly," he muttered, wondering how to open the door.

Then he saw that one of the Baron's rings had a button where the jewel should have been.

There was a loud whirring as Max touched the button. The Baron slid slowly aside to reveal an eerie, wood-panelled passage, lit only by candlelight. There was no one around, so Max and Sally tiptoed in, not knowing what, or who, to expect. It was a bit spooky, but they reached the open door at the end, unchallenged.

They peeped into a deserted room. Sally glanced around nervously. Where had the two visitors gone? She spotted some scattered papers and part of an ancient-looking map on the table.

"Property of Den . . . it must be Denzil Grabbitt," Sally exclaimed, reading the bottom line of writing.

She delved into her rucksack and pulled out Jago's map. She knew it would match Denzil's. Max whipped out his new, mini camera. CLICK and the picture was taken.

"Now we've got a copy of the map and no one will know we've been here," he said, stuffing the camera into his pocket. "Let's go."

Sally was looking at the map. There was still one piece missing, but she was sure the writing would give them a clue to where the treasure was hidden.

The writing on Denzil's map was very strange, but as she stared it began to make sense.

DON'T TURN THE PAGE YET

What is written on the map?

DRAGON'S TEETH ROCKS

Denzil's cottage

TRESPASSERS BEWARE

Property of Denzil

Snake passage

DEMON'S COVE

This belongs to Jago Grabbitt

29

Trapped

There was an ominous scraping sound. A panel opened revealing another room and gloomy passage. Framed in the doorway stood Baron Grabbitt and the Doppel Gang.

"I'll take that," the Baron snarled, snatching the map from Max. "We've been watching you sneaking through the Hall on the TV screen."

Max groaned. Closed circuit television; they should have guessed. He looked around, but they were surrounded with no hope of escape. Sally watched miserably as the lady with orange hair studied their map. At least they still had the camera and film. Spikey grabbed Max and a man called Harry pushed Sally towards the dark passage.

They were marched down a flight of wide, stone stairs and through a huge cave to a long passageway. Harry hurried them straight on, ignoring the tunnels on either side, until they came to seven steep steps.

At the bottom they turned left and carried on into a small, round cave. Even Sally had to duck as she stepped into the low tunnel that twisted down and down. There were more steps, but these were so wet and slippery that Sally, who was trying to memorize their route, lost count.

Finally they came to a small, damp cave where the two men left them tied up. Max wriggled across to some jagged rocks and began to saw at the rope around his wrists. Luckily, it was easy to cut. Meanwhile, Sally had worked out where they were and was trying to find the best route out of the caves, avoiding Grabbitt Hall. Her brilliant memory meant she could picture the map clearly.

DON'T TURN THE PAGE YET

Where are they? Which is the shortest route out, avoiding Grabbitt Hall?

31

Escape through the Tunnels

Sally and Max ran so quickly, they were gasping for breath by the time they reached the Snake Passage. But at least there was no danger of being followed here. The tunnel was so narrow, it was a tight squeeze even for Max and Sally.

At last they came to a wider passage which sloped steeply upwards towards a small wooden door. But as Max fumbled with the catch, they heard footsteps, running. A tall figure loomed suddenly from the dark shadows behind them.

DETECTIVE
INSPECTOR
THOMAS CLIPPER

T. Clipper

Special Undercover Agent

"I thought I'd never catch you," a gruff voice wheezed.

Tom! They were trapped. Max shoved against the door, trying desperately to open it. Then Tom whisked out a plastic identity card.

"We thought…" Sally began.

". . . I was one of the Doppel Gang," Tom finished. "I realized that. I came to rescue you and guessed you would make for here, but I had to go the long way round."

They set off at once for Tom's cottage where he could develop their film. As they scrambled out and made their way through the wood and across the fields, Tom told them the rest of the story.

The Grabbitts made an ingenious plan to hide the treasure until the hunt for it had been called off.

They hid it in the confusing maze of tunnels at Demon's Cove and drew a map to show the hiding place.

But the brothers didn't trust each other so they divided the map into three parts. Each wrote a vital clue on his portion. When they died, the map was forgotten.

I'm very interested in the case of the Indian Queen treasure, as Captain Clipper is my great great great grandfather.

Baron Grabbitt is Denzil's great great grandson. Gloria Goldfinger discovered Denzil's map while going through some of his old books.

I have been trailing the Gang for months, investigating their activities.

This is how the Doppel Gang's hunt for the treasure and for the missing parts of the map began.

Photo Identification

Tom led Sally and Max into a tumbledown barn behind his cottage. They gazed around in amazement. Inside, the barn was transformed into a high-tech office. Tom opened an important-looking box marked "Police File". It was packed with photographs.

"I want you to help with evidence," Tom explained, making Max and Sally feel very important. "Pick out every photo showing members of the Doppel Gang."

Tom disappeared into the darkroom with their film while Max and Sally spread out the photos. He particularly wanted them to identify the two new gang members. At first it seemed impossible, but they soon spotted familiar faces and some which were cleverly disguised. They could also name most of them.

DON'T TURN THE PAGE YET

Find all the photos of the Doppel Gang and name as many as you can.

THE DOPPEL GANG:

BARON GRABBITT Millionaire, Gang leader. Power-crazy, highly dangerous.

GLORIA GOLDFINGER The brains of the Gang. Tall, slim and vain. Can't resist expensive jewellery. Often changes hair colour.

JOHN SMITH Now known as Harry Loimeswolde. (Other aliases: Luigi Macaroni, Angus McHaggis.) Ruthless master of disguise. Small scar on left jaw.

SILAS 'SPIKEY' SCARFACE Expert thief. Left leg shorter than right leg. Scar on right cheek.

EUSTACE WHIMPE The Gang's lawyer. Short, skinny and weedy.

+ TWO RECENT RECRUITS

SWINDELLS
BANK
Lutzdor, Switzerland

NAME : GRABBITT (Baron)
FORENAMES : Brian Archibald
ADDRESS : GRABBITT HALL
Nether Muckle.

ACCOUNT NO : AY 12345

The Missing Link

Tom studied the photos of the two new Gang members and frowned.

"Fingers Golightly and Dinah Might. Notorious villains," he said.

Tom held out the newly-developed print showing the two portions of the treasure map. He locked the barn and led Sally and Max across the garden towards his cottage.

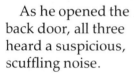

As he opened the back door, all three heard a suspicious, scuffling noise.

They were just in time to see a man disappear through the front door.

Tom glanced across at his safe. It was open and he knew it was empty.

Sally dashed to the window and saw Spikey running towards a van. He was brandishing a small piece of paper. The engine revved, Spikey jumped inside and the van roared away.

Tom lifted down a dusty tin.

"The Doppel Gang must know who I am," he said. "They've taken my copy. But . . . I've still got the original."

Copy? Original? What was Tom talking about? He took a small scrap of yellowing paper from the tin. It was the third piece of the Grabbitt brothers' map.

"But how did you find it?" asked Sally, not quite believing her eyes.

This portion of the map had belonged to Joshua Grabbitt, the youngest of the brothers. For Tom was not only descended from Captain Clipper, but also from Joshua Grabbitt. The Captain's grandson had married Joshua's grandaughter. Just last week, Tom had found the map rolled up and forgotten in the attic along with Captain Clipper's chest. Now they could work out where the treasure was hidden. But they would have to move fast to get there before the Doppel Gang.

DON'T TURN THE PAGE YET

Can you work out where the treasure is hidden?

Treasure from the Indian Queen

They raced out to Tom's jeep and set off. Tom radioed for reinforcements and the jeep lurched down the gravel track. With Max in the lead, they scrambled through the trapdoor and down into the maze of dark tunnels, to the Demon's Lair. The Doppel Gang had yet to arrive.

Large boulders made a screen around one side of the cave. It was impossible to hear anyone approaching because it was high tide and the sound of the sea roaring in the tunnels echoed through the cave. Tom found a good hiding place where they could keep watch. They switched off their torch and waited.

It was not long before Max spotted a torch beam. The Doppel Gang marched into the cave. Harry counted ten paces from the centre and the Gang set to work with spades, while Gloria and the Baron watched.

At last there was a shout, the Gang had found the treasure. It was time to put Tom's plan into action. The special microwave radio crackled to life. As Tom struggled to hear what was being said, he turned very pale and began to look very worried.

"There's been a delay," he whispered. "The plan won't work. We only have enough men to guard one tunnel and there are four exits from the cave."

Sally's mind whizzed into action. She thought back to the plan of the caves and realized there WAS only one way out. Sally, Max and Tom edged their way out of the cave, while the Gang were busy with the chests. Tom radioed his instructions.

DON'T TURN THE PAGE YET

Is Sally right? Which exit should they guard?

The Demon's Eye Diamond

The plan was a success. Almost before Max and Sally knew it, the six members of the Doppel Gang were safely in police custody. Tom, Max and Sally followed as the Gang were led through the tunnels to Demon's Cove, where a police launch was waiting. Outside on the beach, Tom opened the chests. Max and Sally gazed in amazement at the treasure. But they quickly realized something was wrong. The red leather box that should have held the Demon's Eye diamond was empty.

Had one of the Doppel Gang secretly taken it? Sally didn't think so. She was convinced the Grabbitt brothers had never found the famous jewel all those years ago. But if she was right, where was it now? Sally remembered Captain Clipper's logbook, she knew that it held the answer.

DON'T TURN THE PAGE YET

Where is the Demon's Eye diamond?

40

Clues

Answers

Pages 6-7

The message is in morse code. This is what it says:

Diving party landing with equipment and wreckage from Indian Queen. Standby to receive at Demon's Cove. End of message.

Pages 8-9

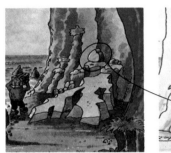 

One thing has changed. The large boulder on top of the ledge has been turned round. It is ringed in both pictures.

Large boulder

Pages 10-11

The letters are written in an old-fashioned way and where the letter s comes in the middle of a word, it is written like an f. Some words are also spelt differently.
This is what it says:

Enter through the trapdoor in the cave above the Cove.

This keyhole symbol shows there is a door.

Beware at high tide when tunnels flood – they be drawn in blue.

Demon's Cove

This belongs to Jago Grabbitt

Snake Passage

Pages 12-13

They open the trapdoor using the metal pole Max knocked over as a lever. They balance the pole on top of the rock which then acts as a pivot.

This means they need less effort and strength to open the door.
These diagrams show how Max and Sally open the trapdoor.

The pole is pushed through the ring

Metal pole lever

Pivot rock

They push here to lift open the trapdoor

Pages 14-15

The trapdoor opens into Tom's cottage. Sally knows this because she spots the stained glass window which she saw from the outside on page 5.

Stained glass window

Pages 16-17

Sally has spotted the name Captain T. Clipper on the sea chest. He was captain of the Indian Queen. You can see the name ringed here.

The other puzzling things Max and Sally have noticed are labelled.

Gun in holster

Powerful binoculars

Radio transceiver

Camera and lenses

Pistol

Pages 18-19

Max saw the man in the photo last night. He was one of the people on the beach at Demon's Cove.

Here is the man from the photo.

Max suspects the Doppel Gang are looking for the lost treasure from the Indian Queen. His main reasons are: the Doppel Gang's interest in ancient treasure; the message Max and Sally decoded on page 7; the fact that

Baron Grabbitt, the Gang leader, has the same surname as the Grabbitt brothers who wrecked the Indian Queen.

Pages 20-21

Max decodes the message using the carved stick that Sally found on page 12. Place the stick below each line of writing. Lines on the stick match the letters on the paper. To break the code, read the letters which are above notches on the stick.

Here is the message:

Emergency meeting of Doppel Gang in 30 minutes. Important new developments. Usual meeting place. Be prompt.

Pages 22-23

The building marked X on the map is ringed in black.

Tom's cottage is here.

Pages 24-25

The safe route into Grabbitt Hall is marked in black.

Pages 26-27

In the painting above the fireplace, Max spotted a door where the life-size portrait of Baron Grabbitt now hangs. The entrance to the hidden passage must be behind this picture.

This is the door Max spotted.

The door is behind this portrait.

Pages 28-29

The words on Denzil's portion of the map are written backwards. This is what it says:

Two Serpents

Go First towards the star.
Go Last towards the moon. Ten paces from the centre, dig one fathom down.

Denzil's cottage

Dragon's Teeth Rocks

Trespassers beware. Property of Denzil Grabbitt

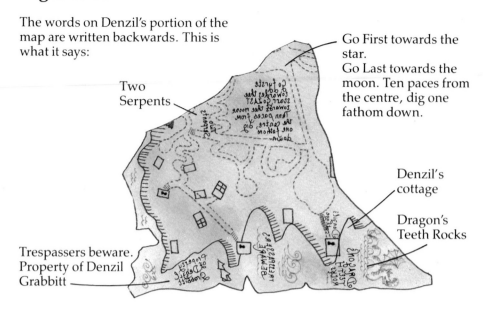

Pages 30-31

The shortest way out is marked in black.

Sally and Max are here.

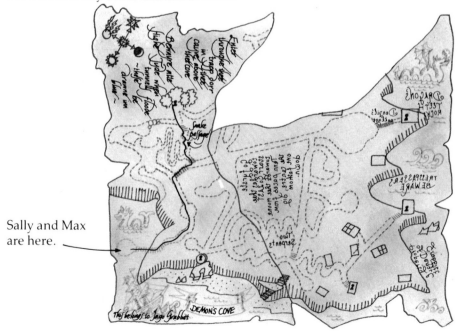

Pages 34-35

Here you can see the members of the Doppel Gang.

Silas 'Spikey' Scarface

Dinah Might

Eustace Whimpe

Gloria Goldfinger

Harry Loimeswolde

Fingers Golightly

Silas 'Spikey' Scarface

Eustace Whimpe

Dinah Might

Fingers Golightly

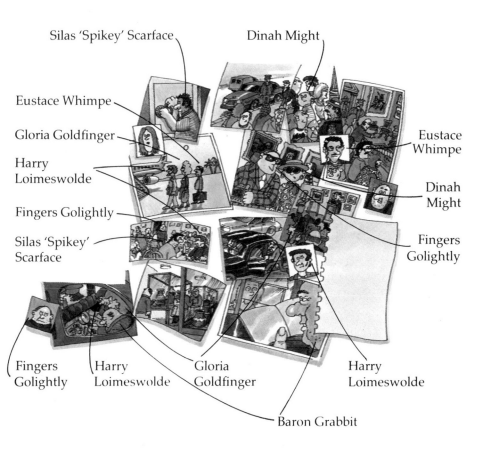

Fingers Golightly

Harry Loimeswolde

Gloria Goldfinger

Harry Loimeswolde

Baron Grabbit

Pages 36-37

Written in order, the clues say:
Enter through the trapdoor in the cave above the Cove. (Map page 11.)
Go First towards the star. (Map page 29.)
Second, look left from the Brigand's Boot and then descend the stair; steer by the comet into the Demon's Lair. (Map page 37.)

Go Last towards the moon. Ten paces from the centre, dig one fathom down. (Map page 29.)

(One fathom is equal to six feet.)

You can see where the treasure is buried on the completed map, shown on the next page.

The treasure is buried here.

The Grabbitt brothers' route to the treasure is marked here in black.

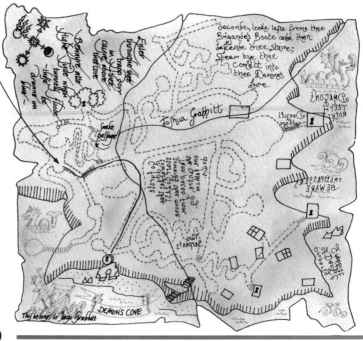

Pages 38-39

Sally is right. This is the only tunnel that must be guarded.

It is high tide and so this tunnel is flooded.

This tunnel is blocked.

This tunnel leads to the Snake Passage. It is too narrow for anyone larger than Sally and Max to squeeze through (see page 32).

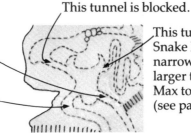

Page 40

Read the last entry in Captain Clipper's logbook on page 19. This tells you the Demon's Eye diamond is hidden in the telescope which Max tries to look through on page 18.

You can see the diamond gleaming here.

First published in 1988 by
Usborne Publishing Ltd,
20 Garrick Street,
London WC2E 9BJ, England.

Copyright © 1988 Usborne Publishing Ltd.

The name Usborne and the device ♔ are
Trade Marks of Usborne Publishing Ltd.